GEMS
—UNLEASHED—

AN ILLUSTRATED STORY
BY DAN KUBISHTA

1st edition, Aug. 2021

ISBN: 978-1-7376840-2-2

Cover design by Dan Kubishta

THE SETTING

A Pacific island known by many names is largely the setting of this story. Its official name is unknown. It has been called over time Brisby, Canby, and Hawaii. Oftentimes referred to as simply The Island, the place has a city with sparkling avenues and towering scrapes, and many different people living there. There are the occasional cargo lines coming and going to offer goods and services, but The Island is mostly self-sufficient.

CHAPTER ONE
THE PALL

"What's that?" asked Paige.

Max looked over.

"What do you mean?"

"That sound," said Paige. "It sounds like crickets."

It was around six o'clock in the evening. The island was lit with lights. Paige was turning into an astute businesswoman. There was no telling her future, but it seemed as bright as her father's. She heard a sound.

"Hello, Colette," she said.

Colette had strolled up to the lawns of Dazing Inn, where Max's aunt ran the place with an iron fist.

"Tell me," said Colette, "Do you not feel in the air something strange?"

"I feel it," said Paige, unraveling the white ribbon that had held her blonde hair together artfully.

2
MR. GREEN'S SUCCESS

"One at a time!" yelled Timothy Green. His gem store was crowded with customers, each one vying for the season's bestselling jewelry. Marco, Mr. Green's business partner, had come across a cache of extremely rare stones. Now, everyone wanted a piece.

"I have stood here for six hours!" proclaimed one woman. "I deserve a ruby."

Then, she broke out in song.

Gems Unleashed

A Ruby,
A Ruby,
All my life I have wanted a ruby
There is no match here
There is no match there, there is no
match anywhere on planet
That comes close to compare
To the miraculous finds
That Marco and Timothy have
uncovered
Now tell me, you fiends
Excuse me, my friends
How you have all discerned
That my lineage is unworthy
To inherit
These stones
Or to buy them, it's perfectly
reasonable
That I will be the recipient
Of such magic ornaments
I can hardly contain my excitement

"Oh please," said a person
standing next to her, rolling their eyes.

3

ABOUT NED

Ned's ear was listening to the ground. There was a faint rumbling, and he stood up, afraid. Across the island, a volcano was erupting. He took two strides forward and two steps back. He was alone, having escaped the clutches of some of his ex-cronies earlier on, and now he could not help but investigate.

4

THE MYSTERY

A team of shrouded figures unearthed a treasure. Around them, lights shone in a flower pattern. Above them, the sky twinkled with stars.

"You fools," came a rasping voice. "You're not doing it right. What have I hired you for?"

Six of the people started walking away, but their master screamed at them.

"No! You cannot leave. You are bound."

"Yes, we are bound. Bound. Bound."

"Zombies," the leader said calmly. "You're all a bunch of miserable zombies."

5
ALDOUS AND TIN

"Dear friend," Aldous said, sipping a drink, "You are positively the coolest law enforcement officer I have ever met."

"Indeed?"

Officer Lieutenant Tin sat across Aldous, or "Aldy" as he affectionately called him, in the tavern known as Melanie's. A parrot flew around the room, flapping its brilliant wings.

"Report, sir!"

It was one of Tin's team.

"Yes, what news?"

The team member stood about three feet away from Tin and Aldous with one hand behind his back. The buttons on his uniform shone, blinding the two.

"There have been reports of misdoing on the east side of the island."

"Misdoing?"

"Aye."

6
THE ASSEMBLAGE

"Kat," said Suzanne. It was Max's mother, talking on the phone to her sister.

"Why have you called today?"

Their relationship had been in the past tumultuous, but in recent times, they had worked to create a friendship.

"Is Max still there?" Suzanne was still attached to her son, sometimes a bit too much, but she meant well and her concerns were always valid.

"Yes. Max is fine. Every time he comes to this island he seems to get involved with trouble, but he always seems to slip out of it."

"That's good to hear."

A violin was playing. Ms. Lilianne Camden sat at a typewriter.

Suddenly, a knock came at the door.

"Who's knocking? Excuse me, Suzanne. There's somebody at the door, and I don't know why they're not using the bell."

She opened the door. In front of her stood a massive man.

"Hello there," he said. "My name's Marco."

"Hello!" Suzanne was flustered.

"I've been dispatched by Mr. Green."

Kat had been friends with Mr. Green for a while, but she had never made her acquaintance with Marco.

"He said he has a special mission," Marco continued, "and he had a certain somebody in mind."

"Yes, what do you mean?"

Marco walked Kat out onto the lawn. Kat's friend, Ms. Rose, was gardening.

"Hello there," she said, her eyelids drooping.

"Hi, miss," Marco said.

"What's going on?"

Max, Paige, Colette, and Gerard were all gathered together.

"What is it that you do?" It was Ms. Rose, talking to Gerard.

"Up until recently, I was a professional musician," said Gerard.

Rose seemed impressed.

"Now, let's get down to business," Marco said. "There have been happenings occurring on the east side of the island. Timothy Green, whom some of you know, has informed me that there is something off. He's been a keen professional for many a year, despite his comedic exterior."

When Marco said "exterior", thunder rolled overhead. On the mountain, the leader of the shrouded figures saw someone approaching. It was Ned.

"Are you listening?" asked Marco. He had once been in the military.

"Yes!" came the staunch reply.

Max knew enough about Marco to know how to act. At a time prior, he had worked for Marco. Finding gems.

Colette stretched, and she and Gerard left together. Paige held her ribbon tightly.

"Why are you telling us all this?" asked Max.

"Of course, there are plenty of other options for me," Marco agreed.

"Why don't you go to the island's army? Will they not help?"

"They will," Marco said, flexing his muscles, "but there are no guarantees that they will succeed."

"This is ridiculous," Kat said, holding a tray of cranberry juice. Marco took a swig and then sat down at a table. Inn guests started arriving, and Kat had to leave to attend to them. Max was trembling. The weight of what was happening had just begun to sink in.

"Your great-grandfather," Max remembered Kat telling him at one point, *"was a valiant man."*

"What's the matter?" Paige asked.

"Remember that necklace we squabbled over?"

"How could I forget?"

"What are you talking about?" asked Marco.

"There was a necklace that my aunt inherited from my great-grandfather. He carried it with him a long time ago."

"And?"

"This necklace was a symbol for him of why he kept going."

The volcano was exploding.

"I was just thinking of how someone could keep going in the face of tremendous adversity."

"You have not seen it," Marco said. "Not yet. None of my men can bring down the power that now belies us."

"Why?" asked Paige.

Kat closed the inn's blinds.

7

THE SONG

THERE IS A PLACE
WAY OFF IN THE EAST
WHERE THERE ARE SHROUDED BEINGS
THEY HAVE HIDDEN IN PLAIN SIGHT
FOR MANY A NIGHT
FOR THAT IS THEIR MODUS OPERANDI
THERE IS NO TELLING
NAY, NO ONE CAN TELL
WHAT WILL BE THEIR NEXT MOVE
HOPEFULLY, THOUGH, KNOCK ON WOOD
OR DOUGH,
THERE WILL BE A SHALLOW
DENOUEMENT

8
NED'S DISCOVERY

Ned hid behind a rock. Ever since he had crossed Aldous Price, he had to make his way on the island in unconventional ways. Aldous Price, it was known, was not only the most famous figure on the island but also the most powerful. Sure, there was Officer Lt. Tin, who held much sway. Sure, there was the matron of the city. Marco and Mr. Green held power as well, but not very much. The military on the island was small.

"Who goes there?" It was the leader of the shrouded figures.

Ned gulped, then ran out from his hiding place. The volcano's lava was flowing, but it formed in benign pools at the bottom. The city was not in danger.

"Who are you?"

The figure did not answer. There was a truck parked nearby, and inside of the truck were more figures.

Ned looked at his watch.

"Not a good time to tell the time," the leader said sarcastically. Ned was captured and thrown into the truck. Once inside, he looked around. He was surrounded by fools.

"I will once more become king of the jungle," said the leader.

Ned ripped back the leader's hood.

"Lion," he said.

"Hear me roar," came the reply.

9

THE ROLLS-ROYCE

"So," Tin was saying. "We have abandoned my vehicle for the sake of a Price's. Isn't it cruise liners you normally deal in?"

Aldous looked out the window. His driver, Jay, was taking them to a mining operation outside of the city. Mr. Green was also in the car.

"Old friend," said Mr. Price, "this car is golden."

They arrived.

"If everything goes according to plan," said Mr. Green, "Marco should be here within the hour. Look! There's his beloved mule."

10

NED SHOWS HIS QUALITY

"I know jiu-jitsu, you know."

"Ned! You are a nobody. You're just like me. At one time on track to becoming a rising star, close to the Price company...now look. Razed to the ground! Both of us, well maybe not so much me."

Lion laughed.

"How did you escape?"

Lion stood on top of the truck.

"It was not hard, weirdly enough. To get back to my point, though, you are a fool. Once believing yourself to be the next Aldous, phony crown and all, you have made nothing of yourself."

Ned's copper tufts of hair drooped like a dying plant. The group around him chided him.

Ned, Ned, the simpleton
You cannot hold a job
You try your best
Lest you get arrested
For being a cowardly fiend
Let us attest
To your absolute restlessness
You complete quack of a being
Ned, Ned, the simpleton
What a joke we now behold
For we are the masters
Of the island of Canby
And Ned?
You're getting old

"Enough!" Ned cried.

The smoke of the volcano was billowing.

In the valley, Marco, Max, and Paige arrived at the mining quarry. Tin looked towards the east, his grey mustache bristling.

At the city's largest port, a cruise liner was arriving. Its name was Anne, and she was helmed by a certain captain Lawrence.

Running from the ship, Lawrence passed through the exiting crowd, calling a taxi.

"We are getting more help," said Aldous, putting down a cell phone.

"Listen!" said Paige. "Do you hear it?"

"Enough!"

It was Ned's voice, echoing down into the valley. Ned cracked his knuckles. "Do not mock me," he said with a belligerent tone. Lion revealed a box of gems.

"Check it out," he said with an alluring tone.

For a moment, Ned was caught off guard.

"These are the gems that are so rare," he said as if hypnotized, "they were found on the island and sold at Timothy Green's shop."

"Yes," said Lion.

"No!" said Ned. "I will not be bought."

He swung a punch. The gems scattered. The cronies collected the gems, stashing them into their pockets.

"No!" said Lion. He revved up the truck.

"What is happening," Ned said, laughing in disbelief.

At the island's park, Ms. Rose was selling the roses she had just harvested. Everything was so completely normal that it almost hurt. People strolled around the lawns with propriety. No one was aware of the happenings on the east side of the island.

11
THE GOOD TEAM

"Now listen," said Tin. "There has been talk of misdoing on the island. It has long been said that there is corruption, but now we have leads."

"This is ridiculous," said Mr. Green. "Petty thieves and hooligans, nothing more."

"It may be!" retorted Tin, "But there is nothing more disheartening to me than the degradation of my beloved island. Without further ado, I will call your names, and you shall reply with *here*."

Above him, vultures flew in circles. Mule the Jule made a braying noise.

"Paige Price!"

"Here."

"Aldous Price!"

"Here."

"Max...what's your last name?"

"Holloway," said Max. "Here."

"Timothy Green!"

"Here!"

"Captain Lawrence!"

"Here!"

"Colette Price?"

"She could not make the appointment," said Paige. Her ribbon was tied neatly in her hair.

"Gerard Frist!"

"Also, could not make the appointment."

Tin sighed.

"Marco Mix!"

"Here." He shook Mr. Green's hand.

Tin looked over the bunch. "It is a makeshift team," he said, "but it needs to be. To be undercover in such an unlikely way, that is what my military cannot do."

12

THE PLANS GO OUT THE WINDOW

"Here's the plan," began Aldous.

"No," said Tin, "I must relay it."

A truck drove past. The group fell silent. Ned was peering out the window of the truck, waving.

"Ned?" said Paige.

"Good riddance," said Aldous, "That fool is still about?"

Ned rolled the window down.

"It's them! It's them! I've found the miscreants!"

Tin blinked.

13

Rose and Libby

Libby walked up to the flower stand.

"Good afternoon," she said.

"Hello, Libby," said Ms. Rose. "You may clock in."

Libby took a punch card.

14

THE PARKING LOT

"Into the Rolls Royce!" yelled Aldous. They all piled in.

"Follow that truck, Jay."

Jay turned the radio on.

"This will be interesting," Paige commented, folding the cuffs of her white blouse.

The truck sped along. Lion was trying to figure out where to go next, and he decided upon the Hotel Empress.

"You've got to be kidding me," Max said.

Inside the hotel, the front desk clerk sat quietly. She wore a tie, and her hair was slicked back in a bun.

The truck pulled up. Ned stepped out, and soon after, the cronies did as well. They walked up to the woman at the front desk.

"Hello," said Lion. He looked a bit disheveled, as did his team. Ned wanted to be anywhere other than where he was.

Tin stepped out of the car. Aldous stepped out of the car. Paige stepped out of the car, putting sunglasses on. Max stepped out of the car. Jay stayed inside the car. Mr. Green stayed inside the car. Marco stepped out of the car.

"As you were," he said.

Finally, the captain stepped out of the car.

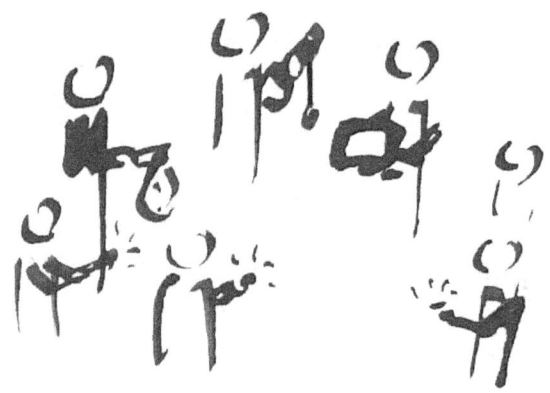

15.
THE SEVEN GEM TRADERS

"Do you want to know what we are up to?" Lion asked.

The group was sitting in the hotel lobby. Their dress was pedestrian, but their motives remained hidden.

"I don't really care," said Ned.

"Yes," said Lion. "You should, though."

"Ha!"

"Now you're laughing?"

The lady at the front desk glanced over.

"There is a legend here on this island about the seven gem dealers."

"The seven gem dealers?"

"Yes. Are you familiar with it?"

"I can't say that I am, jungle cat."

"What did you call me?"

"You're a piccolo, Lion. A complete and utter piccolo. I don't ever normally like to roll with your type 'o cat."

"Quiet," said Lion. He got up. "Walk this way."

The group followed him. Ned was sitting, stubborn as Jules the mule.

"Ned," said Lion, "I am not trying to harm you."

Ned got up and followed. Lion led them to a courtyard at the back of the hotel. There were beautiful blossoms and flowing fountains.

Lion spoke. "The story goes that there were seven gem traders. These traders lived here on the island long before any settlers came to inhabit its shores. They were incredibly astute, so much so that their bloodline flourishes today."

Timothy Green Ned thought.

34

"The seven gem traders were eventually forced to expand their business model overseas, but not before they had established deep connections with every single business person on the island."

Lion stopped. The sound of the fountains was crisp.

"Tell me more," said Ned.

"The bread crumb trail ends after their death," Lion admitted. "I researched for seven years."

16

THE PARTY IS CRASHED

A voice was heard, coming from the ballroom. Lion's ears perked up.

BRISTOL'S GREEN EYES HAD BEEN FULL OF SURPRISE

SINCE THAT EVENING IN TRUE BLUE NOVEMBER

THEN SHE HAD BEEN COVERED
WITH A VEIL AND A FLOWER
WITH THE HOPE THAT SHE WOULD BE
HIDDEN

The cronies were intrigued.

"What a beautiful sound," one said.

Paige? Ned wondered.

One by one, the entire team that had been assembled by the likes of Marco and Mr. Green walked into the courtyard. They surrounded the group, and Ned's forehead dripped with sweat.

"Hello, there," said Tin.

"Hello, officer," said Lion. Then, he saw Aldous.

"You've brought the whole group."

There were rays of light shining down from the windows installed above the courtyard. Outside, the clouds had passed over, working now their machinations above the island's north shore.

"We are just seeing what's going on," said Tin politely. "We have heard of strange happenings upon the island."

"Indeed," said Lion,

"What is your name," demanded Marco.

"Lion. I am an open book."

"Is that your real name?"

"Of course not. I would not say my real name unless I had no other choice."

"Well, you *have* no other choice," said Paige.

17

COLETTE, GERARD, AND THE CAT OF DAZING INN

"Meow," said Colette, looking at Kat's cat.

"Do not touch her," Gerard said ominously. "She will not take it fondly."

"I just want to boop her nose."

"I wouldn't," said Gerard.

"You're probably right," said Colette.

She gathered dishes up from the sink that she had been washing them in, and put them above in wooden cupboards. Lilianne Camden entered the area where the two were, the common area of the inn.

"Reports from downtown," said Lilianne.

"There's been an uprising."

18

BENJAMIN BRANDY

THERE ONCE WAS A MAN
WHO WENT BY THE NAME
OF BENJAMIN
THAT WAS HIS TITLE
EVERY JULY HE WOULD TIE UP HIS TIE
AND PROMENADE NEXT TO THE SHORE
THERE WAS A YOUNG WOMAN

WHO STOOD ALSO WITH HIM, SOMETIMES
IF SHE WASN'T TOO BORED
HER NAME WAS CECILE,
AND SHE WAS AN AMERICAN
WITH ALL OF THE TRAPPINGS THAT
ENSUES,
WITH RIBBONS AND HEELS AND GEMS
'ROUND HER FINGERS
SHE DIDN'T LOOK TERRIBLY POOR

"A solid poem," said Benjamin Brandy.

He was writing about his father. He took the quill of a feathered pen and dipped it in ink.

"What century are we in?" asked his female colleague.

"Here, time stops," came the reply.

He was sitting almost directly above where Lion now faced a confrontation with the unlikely army, in a room set aside as a private suite for the famous author Mr. Benjamin Brandy.

"I've written it in twenty seconds," he boasted with an ounce of earnestness.

"Yes, we all know you are a great wordsmith, but can you do something worthy of true honor?"

"How dare you, Frida. I am a respected man, I write books of poetry and on the weekends I help with the fire brigade. I am well-rounded, although sometimes I do like to imbibe."

"Hence your name."

"Correct. Now, about your last point, there is absolutely no evidence for your ridiculous claim. I am the master of my own universe, and I do what I want. Pardon me, that is not true to form! What am I blabbering on about."

"Start again, and maybe tonight we shall play bocce in the park."

Benjamin cleared his throat.

"I am Benjamin Brandy, son of Benjamin Brandy, and I am the living manifestation of a gentleman. There is no one that can surpass my excellence in everything."

Frida laughed.

"I am Benjamin Brandy, the most incredible person to ever, ever, ever, ever, live."

"Do not do that," Frida said.

"Do what?" Benjamin replied.

The phone in the room rang off its hook. Frida picked it up.

"Yes?"

It was the front desk lady.

"Hello, yes. I don't mean to intrude, but there is an emergency in the courtroom. We are asking all occupants to evacuate the premises."

"So be it," was the reply.

19
THE PLOT THICKENS

Paige stepped forward.

"Again being rash," Aldous said.

"Who's that girl?"

Ned took a step backyard, yawning.

Tin's cell phone rang. He answered it. After listening for a moment, he hung it up.

"Who was that?"

"A dispatcher. There seems to be a problem downtown. I must leave."

Lion and his men moved now in circular motions around the unlikely army.

"Where's Mr. Green?"

"Where *is* Mr. Green."

Timothy was jogging out in the parking lot. Jay was inside the air-conditioned Rolls-Royce still, but the gem smith had left not five minutes earlier. He met Benjamin Brandy and Frida in the parking lot as the place was evacuated.

"What's new?" Benjamin asked.

"No time to talk, friend," said Mr. Green. "I have business that needs to be attended to."

20
THE CLOCKTOWER

The island's clocktower chimed. It was three 'o clock in the afternoon, and the city was in disarray. Tin arrived downtown soon after, and the uprising was resolved.

In the park, Ms. Rose and Libby conducted business in the most professional manner possible. There was not a dissatisfied customer that day, and decorated roses were seen everywhere.

"I can't wait for the next gala," said Libby. "Hopefully, I can go to it this time around."

"You've had such a go of it here," said Ms. Rose, "why don't you go back to corporate life?"

"Yes, there is peril on the island, but still, I think I have found a home here."

Ms. Rose hugged Libby. She almost shed a tear.

21
THE OFFER

Max stepped forward. Grabbing a potted plant, he moved to fight one of the mysterious figures.

"Would you like some chocolate?" one of them said.

Nobody knew what to say.

"No," said Paige, "Maybe. I don't know, what kind?"

"Tadbury's and Lindon," was the answer.

"No," said Paige. "It's poison."

The figure's hand withdrew the candy.

"Alright!" said Aldous. "Enough monkey business. There are answers that need to be revealed, and this will be the day they are revealed unless my intention is spoiled!"

Ned combed his hair. He stayed his distance from Aldous, although he also was still proud enough to be completely at ease with his presence.

"There is a story," began Lion, "Of the seven gem traders…"

"Not this again!"

All of a sudden, the light from the ceiling was extinguished. Someone had pulled a cover over the windows, and the courtyard was black as pitch. Paige threw off her heels and put on boots. Then, a small bird flew through the courtyard. In its beak it held an envelope, and the envelope dropped to the floor. Lion took it, opened it, and read the note inside.

"Pigeon mail," he snarled.

"What does it say?" Marco demanded.

Lion brought out a lighter.

"Don't burn it!" said Aldous.

"Why?" asked Lion.

"You know why," Aldous retorted.

"Why, why, why. Why, why, why, why, why, why, why."

"Do not say anything more, Lion...or as they call you on the mainland, Liam."

Lion laughed.

"I almost forgot. You know my real name."

22

The End, Part I

"I know your real name," said Aldous. "I knew your parents."

The figures shuddered. Paige removed her earrings.

"What is all of this nonsense," said Max. "A conspiracy, a mystery, a group of outlier miscreants. I want answers."

"As do I," said Paige.

"As do I," said Colette.

"It was just an altercation," said Liliane Camden. "Nothing to fret."

Colette sat down on a couch next to Gerard. The cat hissed.

"Where's Paige and Max?

"What's it going to be?" said Lion as he burned the envelope containing the note.

"That's it," Mr. Price said.

The captain was wearing his uniform. On his uniform were six medals. The figures surrounded him, stripped him of the medals, and all stepped back in unison. Paige gasped.

ONE
TWO
THREE
ONE
TWO
THREE

The captain ran forward, his eyes blazing. Mr. Green threw a briefcase at

Lion. Paige was hoisted up to the ceiling by a harness that she had been unwillingly strapped into by three of the figures. Max wept.

23

THE END, PT II

Rose collected a bouquet of tiger lilies.

"Follow me," she called to Colette.

Colette smiled. The two loaded six pails of flowers into Rose's white shining car. They drove up to the Hotel Empress, where they found a crowd of people lingering outside. The sun was beginning to sink into the west, and the island felt a cold chill. Lion emerged from the hotel dressed like a lawyer.

"What happened?" asked Rose. She was talking to the lady at the front desk.

"I don't know," she said. Her leopard-print blouse was buttoned up to her collar.

Max shined his shoes.

ONE
TWO
THREE
ONE
TWO
THREE

Marco let seven punches fall. The figures were razed to the ground.

"Paige," said Max.

"Yes," she answered.

"I think I might have made a mistake leaving the mainland, no?"

"There are no mistakes," said Paige. "Only lessons learned."

Next to the hotel was a natural park. A peacock walked on a bench.

Below it, tigers wrestled with each other playfully. Benjamin Brandy and Frida watched.

"I wonder what was happening that we had to leave the hotel?" Benjamin mused.

"Yes, I have no idea," Frida said sadly.

ONE
TWO
THREE
ONE
TWO
THREE

"I have something to say," said Max. The figures were on the floor.

"Make it quick, buddy," Marco reminded him.

"There is nothing I can say to remedy what has happened today. I know there are forces that are beyond my control at work. However, there is something that I think I can offer. A solution, as they call it."

Max said what he had to say, and the conspiracy was unraveled. Not by his doing alone, but by the team that had been assembled for the task.

The ocean shimmered. Ned was talking on the phone. Gerard, Colette, Max, and Paige were sitting on the deck of a cruise liner.

"Constance is such a pretty boat," Paige beamed.

The sun was setting. There was a slight breeze that swept through the palm trees of the island.

"Well," said Max, "the day was won."

"Don't be so sure," said Paige.

She walked up to Constance's viewing deck.

"What do you see up there, Paige?"

"A sunset," she said.

GEMS UNLEASHED

Dan Kubishta lives and works on the West Coast, U.S.A. *Gems Unleashed* is his fifth book.